MW01674395

The Dancing Shoes

by Liza Moonlight

Original Title:

The Dancing Shoes

Copyright© Creative Arts Management OÜ All rights Reserved.

ISBN 978-9916-722-26-8

Once upon a time, in a faraway kingdom, there lived a young and beautiful girl named Isadora. She was the daughter of a humble shoemaker who made the most exquisite shoes in the land. Isadora was known to be an excellent dancer and would spend most of her days twirling and leaping around in her father's workshop while he worked on his creations.

One day, the king of the kingdom announced a grand ball, and everyone in the land was invited. Isadora was overjoyed at the news and begged her father to make her the most beautiful pair of dancing shoes in the kingdom.

Her father agreed, and for weeks, he worked tirelessly to create the perfect pair of dancing shoes for his daughter. Finally, the day of the ball arrived, and Isadora put on the beautiful shoes her father had made for her. As soon as she stepped onto the dance floor, everyone was mesmerized by her grace and beauty. She twirled and spun around the ballroom, her feet barely touching the ground.

Isadora felt like she was flying, and everyone who watched her dance felt the same way.

But as the night wore on, Isadora noticed that her shoes began to feel tight. At first, she thought it was just because she had been dancing for so long, but soon the pain became unbearable. She tried to take off her shoes, but they wouldn't budge.

The shoes seemed to have a life of their own and refused to come off her feet.

Isadora panicked and ran out of the ballroom, still wearing her shoes. She ran as fast as she could, but the shoes seemed to be pulling her back. She stumbled and fell, and as she hit the ground, the shoes began to dance on their own, dragging Isadora along with them.

Isadora realized that the shoes were cursed and that she would never be able to take them off. She tried everything she could think of, but nothing worked. The shoes kept dancing, dragging her along wherever they pleased.

Days turned into weeks, and weeks turned into months, but the shoes never stopped dancing.

Isadora became weak and tired, and her feet were covered in blisters and sores. She longed for the days when she could dance for fun and not because the shoes forced her to.

One day, Isadora came across a wise old woman who lived deep in the forest. The old woman had heard of the cursed shoes and knew exactly how to break the curse.

She told Isadora that she had to dance in the shoes until they were completely worn out.

Isadora was hesitant at first, but she knew she had to do whatever it took to break the curse. She put on the shoes and began to dance. The shoes were heavy and uncomfortable, but Isadora danced on.

Dracul thought for a moment, then grinned. "A pencil!" he exclaimed.

The wizard nodded. "Well done, young dragon. You have proven yourself worthy of a few spells." He taught Dracul a few basic spells, and the dragon was thrilled to learn them. She danced through pain and exhaustion, through rain and sunshine, through joy and sorrow.

Years went by, and Isadora never stopped dancing. The shoes became tattered and worn, and finally, one day, they fell off her feet. Isadora fell to the ground, exhausted but relieved. She had broken the curse, and she was finally free.

Isadora returned to her village, and everyone was amazed to see her again. She was no longer the young girl they remembered.

She had grown into a wise and mature woman who had endured a great deal of hardship. Isadora's father was overjoyed to see his daughter again, and together they continued to make the most beautiful shoes in the land.

Isadora never forgot the lessons she had learned while wearing the cursed shoes.

She knew that sometimes, you have to dance through pain and hardship to find freedom and happiness.

She continued to dance, but now it was by choice, and the joy she felt was more profound than ever before. And so, Isadora lived happily, inspiring others to dance through their pain and find the beauty in life.

But he struggled to turn into bigger animals, like a bear or an elephant. It seemed like the spell was too powerful for him to handle.

The wizard noticed Dracul's frustration and sat him down. "You are trying too hard," he said. "The spell requires patience and focus. You must let it come to you naturally."

Years went by, and Isadora's reputation as a wise and skilled shoemaker grew, just as her fame as a dancer had in her youth. People from far and wide came to her to have shoes made that would perfectly fit their feet and suit their needs. She would spend long hours in her workshop, crafting each pair of shoes with great care and attention to detail, and many were the stories she heard from her clients while they waited.

One day, a young woman came to her workshop, looking for a pair of shoes that would help her to dance with grace and elegance. The woman's name was Sabrina, and she was a member of the court of the king, who was a great lover of dance.

Isadora was struck by Sabrina's beauty and grace and decided to make her the most exquisite pair of dancing shoes she had ever made.

She spent many days working on them, putting all her skill and artistry into every stitch.

Finally, the shoes were ready, and Sabrina put them on, eager to show them off at the next royal ball. As soon as she started to dance, the courtiers were amazed. They had never seen such grace and beauty in a dancer before.

Sabrina twirled and spun around the ballroom, her feet barely touching the ground.

The king was so impressed that he asked Sabrina to become the principal dancer of the royal court. She accepted the offer, and soon she was dancing every night, wearing the shoes that Isadora had made for her.

But as the weeks went by, Sabrina began to notice that her feet were hurting. At first, she thought it was just a minor discomfort, but soon the pain became unbearable. She tried to take off the shoes, but they wouldn't budge. The shoes seemed to have a life of their own and refused to come off her feet.

Sabrina panicked and ran out of the ballroom, still wearing her shoes. She ran as fast as she could, but the shoes seemed to be pulling her back. She stumbled and fell, and as she hit the ground, the shoes began to dance on their own, dragging Sabrina along with them.

Isadora heard of Sabrina's plight and went to see her.

She recognized the shoes immediately and knew that they were cursed, just like the ones she had worn many years before.

She told Sabrina the story of her own cursed shoes and how she had broken the curse by dancing until the shoes were worn out.

Sabrina was hesitant at first, but she knew she had to do whatever it took to break the curse.

She put on the shoes and began to dance. The shoes were heavy and uncomfortable, but Sabrina danced on.

She danced through pain and exhaustion, through rain and sunshine, through joy and sorrow.

Months went by, and Sabrina never stopped dancing. The shoes became tattered and worn, and finally, one day, they fell off her feet.

Sabrina fell to the ground, exhausted but relieved. She had broken the curse, and she was finally free.

From that day on, Sabrina danced with more joy and grace than ever before. She knew that she had been given a great gift by Isadora, who had taught her the importance of perseverance and the power of dancing with a free and joyful heart.

And so, Sabrina and Isadora continued to dance and make shoes, each in their own way, inspiring others to dance through their pain and find the beauty in life, just like the shoes they had worn. And they lived happily ever after, spreading joy and love wherever they went.

The Snow Queen

by Liza Moonlight

Once upon a time, in a far-off kingdom, there lived a beautiful young girl named Elsa. Elsa had skin as white as snow, hair as black as ebony, and eyes as blue as sapphires. Her beauty was so extraordinary that everyone who saw her was captivated by her grace and charm.

One day, when Elsa was wandering through the forest, she stumbled upon a mirror lying on the ground. The mirror was unlike any other mirror she had ever seen. It was made of pure ice and reflected everything with extraordinary clarity.

Intrigued by the mirror, Elsa picked it up and took it home with her.

As she examined the mirror more closely, Elsa realized that it had a strange power. Whenever she looked into the mirror, it showed her the darkest aspects of her soul. Elsa was frightened by what she saw and decided to hide the mirror in the attic.

Days passed, and winter arrived in the kingdom.

The snow began to fall, and the wind began to howl, and the people of the kingdom huddled together in their homes. But despite the harsh winter weather, Elsa felt a strange pull toward the attic where she had hidden the mirror.

One night, as she climbed the stairs to the attic, Elsa noticed that the mirror had changed.

It no longer reflected her darkest aspects but instead showed her an image of a beautiful queen with skin as white as snow, hair as black as ebony, and eyes as blue as sapphires, just like Elsa herself.

Elsa was entranced by the image and reached out to touch the mirror. As soon as her finger touched the ice, she was sucked into the mirror and found herself in a beautiful palace made of ice.

The palace was inhabited by a beautiful woman who introduced herself as the Snow Queen. She was the queen of the winter kingdom, and her beauty was beyond compare. Elsa was awestruck by the Snow Queen's grace and charm and felt an immediate kinship with her.

As they talked, Elsa learned that the Snow Queen had been trapped in the mirror for many years and that she needed Elsa's help to break the curse that had been placed upon her. Elsa was eager to help and promised to do whatever it took to free the Snow Queen.

The Snow Queen explained that the only way to break the curse was to find the shards of a magical mirror that had been scattered across the kingdom.

Once all the shards were gathered together, the curse would be broken, and the Snow Queen would be free.

Elsa set out on a journey to find the shards of the magical mirror. She traveled through dark forests, over icy mountains, and across frozen lakes.

Along the way, she met many strange and interesting characters, including a friendly reindeer,
a group of mischievous gnomes, and a brave young prince.

With their help, Elsa found all the shards of the magical mirror and brought them back to the Snow Queen's palace. As soon as the shards were assembled, the curse was broken, and the Snow Queen was freed.

Overjoyed, the Snow Queen thanked Elsa for her help and promised to make her a princess of the winter kingdom. Elsa was thrilled by the offer and accepted it eagerly. She spent many happy years in the winter kingdom, ruling alongside the Snow Queen and bringing warmth and joy to the cold winter months.

But even as she lived in the winter kingdom, Elsa could not help but feel a longing for the world outside. She missed her family, her friends, and the warmth of the sun. So one day, she said goodbye to the Snow Queen and left the winter kingdom to return to her own world.

As she traveled back through the forests and mountains and lakes, Elsa realized that the journey had changed her.

She had learned a lot about herself and the world during her time in the winter kingdom. Elsa now saw the world through different eyes, and she felt a sense of gratitude for everything she had.

When Elsa finally arrived back in her own kingdom, she was greeted with open arms. Her family and friends were overjoyed to see her again, and she told them all about her adventure in the winter kingdom.

As time passed, Elsa became known as the Snow Queen, and her story spread throughout the land.

People from all over the kingdom came to hear her tale, and she became a symbol of hope and courage.

But despite her fame, Elsa remained humble and grateful for all that she had. She continued to live her life with kindness and compassion, always striving to make the world a better place.

And though she never forgot the Snow Queen or the lessons she had learned in the winter kingdom, Elsa knew that her true home was with the people she loved.

And so, the Snow Queen's tale became a legend that was passed down from generation to generation. It taught people to be brave in the face of adversity, to follow their hearts, and to always be grateful for the things they had. And in the end, it was the Snow Queen's courage and kindness that had saved her and made her a hero in the eyes of all who knew her.

The moral of the Snow Queen fairy tale

- Overcoming personal struggles: The Snow Queen represents the dark side of ourselves that we try to hide from others. The Snow Queen's journey to overcome her curse can be seen as a metaphor for overcoming our personal struggles and finding the courage to seek help and support.

- Finding strength in diversity: Elsa's journey takes her to a winter kingdom that is vastly different from her own, yet she finds a sense of belonging and purpose there. The Snow Queen's tale can remind us of the importance of embracing diversity and finding strength in our differences.

- Helping others: Elsa's decision to help the Snow Queen even though it meant leaving her own world behind can be seen as an example of selflessness and empathy. The Snow Queen's story can inspire us to look beyond our own needs and help others in need.

- Gratitude and humility: Even after achieving great things, Elsa remains humble and grateful for what she has. The Snow Queen's tale can remind us to be grateful for the people and things we have in our lives and to live with humility and kindness towards others.

The Wizard's Tower

by Liza Moonlight

Once upon a time, in a land far, far away, there lived a young dragon named Dracul. Dracul was different from the other dragons in his village; he was more interested in books than in hoarding treasure or breathing fire. He spent most of his days reading in the library, dreaming of adventure and magic.

One day, while reading a book about wizards and their magical towers, Dracul felt a strange sensation in his belly. He knew in that moment that he had to find the wizard's tower, no matter what it took.

Dracul set out on his journey, flying over mountains and valleys, through forests and over rivers.

He searched far and wide for the wizard's tower, asking everyone he met if they had seen it. But no one had even heard of it.

After many days of searching, Dracul finally came across an old wizard who knew of the tower's whereabouts. "The wizard's tower is in the Forbidden Forest," said the old wizard.

"But beware, young dragon, for the forest is full of dangerous creatures and treacherous paths."

Dracul thanked the old wizard and set off towards the Forbidden Forest. As he flew over the canopy of trees, he saw all sorts of creatures lurking below. There were trolls, goblins, and even a few unicorns.

Dracul finally spotted the wizard's tower, standing tall and proud in the center of the forest. He flew closer and saw that the tower was surrounded by a moat filled with fiery lava. He knew he had to be careful if he wanted to get inside.

Dracul circled the tower, looking for a way in. He spotted a small window on the top floor and decided to try his luck.

He flew up to the window and peeked inside. There, sitting at a desk, was the wizard himself.

The wizard was an old man with a long white beard and a pointy hat. He was hunched over his desk, scribbling something on a piece of parchment. Dracul cleared his throat to get the wizard's attention.

The wizard looked up and was surprised to see a dragon at his window. "What do you want, young dragon?" he asked.

"I've come to ask you a question," replied Dracul. "How do I become a wizard like you?" The wizard laughed. "You cannot become a wizard, young dragon. Wizards are born, not made."

Dracul was disappointed. "But I've always wanted to be a wizard," he said.

The wizard looked at Dracul for a moment, then smiled. "I'll tell you what, young dragon. If you can answer my riddle, I'll teach you a few spells."

Dracul agreed, eager to learn from the wizard. "What's the riddle?" he asked.

The wizard leaned back in his chair and stroked his beard. "I am taken from a mine, and shut up in a wooden case, from which I am never released, and yet I am used by almost every person. What am I?"

Dracul thought for a moment, then grinned. "A pencil!" he exclaimed.

The wizard nodded. "Well done, young dragon. You have proven yourself worthy of a few spells." He taught Dracul a few basic spells, and the dragon was thrilled to learn them.

Dracul spent the next few weeks at the wizard's tower, learning everything he could from the old man. He learned how to create fireballs, how to levitate objects, and how to turn invisible.

One day, the wizard called Dracul into his study. "I have one last spell to teach you, young dragon," he said.

Dracul's eyes widened with excitement. "What is it?" he asked eagerly.

"It's called the Transformation spell," replied the wizard. "It allows you to transform into any creature you wish. But be warned, young dragon, it is a difficult spell to master, and it comes with great responsibility."

Dracul nodded solemnly. "I understand, and I am ready to learn."

The wizard smiled, and they began their lessons. For days, Dracul practiced the Transformation spell, trying to master it. He turned into a rabbit, a squirrel, a fish, and even a butterfly.

But he struggled to turn into bigger animals, like a bear or an elephant. It seemed like the spell was too powerful for him to handle.

The wizard noticed Dracul's frustration and sat him down. "You are trying too hard," he said. "The spell requires patience and focus. You must let it come to you naturally."

Dracul took the wizard's advice and relaxed. He closed his eyes and focused on the spell. Suddenly, he felt a strange sensation in his body, as if his bones were shifting and changing.

He opened his eyes and saw that he had transformed into a majestic unicorn. His scales had turned into fur, and he had a long horn protruding from his forehead.

He neighed in delight and pranced around the room, amazed at his new form. The wizard smiled, pleased with Dracul's progress.

"You have done well, young dragon," said the wizard. "You have learned all that I can teach you. Now it is up to you to use your powers wisely and for the greater good."

Dracul nodded, feeling grateful for the wizard's guidance. He thanked the old man and took off into the sky, eager to explore his new abilities.

As he flew over the forest, Dracul noticed a group of goblins attacking a small village. He landed and transformed into a bear, using his newfound strength to defeat the goblins and save the village.

From that day forward, Dracul became known as the protector of the land. He used his magical powers to help those in need, and he lived happily ever after.

And the wizard's tower remained a place of magic and wonder, inspiring young dragons like Dracul to pursue their dreams and reach for the stars.

Years passed, and Dracul continued to use his powers for good. He had become a legendary figure in the land, known far and wide as a hero and a friend to all.

One day, as he flew over the forest, he heard a voice calling out to him. It was the wizard, who had grown old and frail.

"Dracul, my old friend," said the wizard. "I have something important to tell you."

Dracul landed beside the wizard, concerned. "What is it?" he asked.
The wizard looked up at him with kind eyes. "I am nearing the end of my life," he said. "And I must pass on my powers to someone else. Someone who is worthy and brave, just like you."

Dracul's heart raced with excitement. "Me?" he asked, hardly daring to believe it.

The wizard nodded. "Yes, you. You have proven yourself time and time again, Dracul. And I have no doubt that you will use your powers wisely and for the greater good."

Dracul bowed his head in gratitude. "Thank you," he said. "I will do my best to live up to your expectations."

The wizard placed a hand on Dracul's shoulder. "I know you will, my friend," he said. "And I am proud to have known you."

With those words, the wizard closed his eyes and breathed his last breath. Dracul stayed by his side, mourning the loss of his mentor and friend.
But he also knew that it was his responsibility to carry on the wizard's legacy.

He took a deep breath and felt the power of the Transformation spell coursing through his veins.

And he knew that he was ready. Ready to take on the world and make it a better place, one act of kindness and bravery at a time.

As he soared into the sky, Dracul looked down at the wizard's tower, now empty and silent. But he knew that the magic of the tower would live on, carried within his heart and the hearts of all those who believed in the power of hope and love.

And with that thought, he flew off into the horizon, ready to face whatever challenges lay ahead.

CPSIA information can be obtained
at www.ICGtesting.com
Printed in the USA
LVHW042007310323
743149LV00004B/290

9 789916 722268